Little
Red Riding Hood

Retold by: Vaijayanti Savant Tonpe

Illustrated by: Santhosh Ramakrishnan

MSM
PRESS

Once upon a time there was a good natured little girl. Her grandmother loved her very much. She was always giving the child presents. Once she made her a small red velvet coat with a hood. The little girl liked it so much she was always wearing it. So people started calling her Little Red Riding Hood.

One day her mother said, "Little Red Riding Hood, take this cake and bottle of medicine to your grandmother. She is sick and weak, and this will give her strength. Go early before it becomes hot. When you are in the woods, be nice and good and don't stray from the path, otherwise you'll fall and break the bottle, and your grandmother will get nothing.

And when you enter her room, don't forget to say good morning, and don't go peeping in all the corners."

"I'll do just as you say," Little Red Riding Hood promised her mother.

Little Red Riding Hood's grandmother lived in the forest, half an hour's walk from the village. As soon as Little Red Riding Hood entered the forest, she met a wolf. However, Little Red Riding Hood did not know that he was a wicked sort of an animal. So she was not afraid of him.

"Good day, Little Red Riding Hood," he said.

"Good day, wolf."

"Where are you going so early, Little Red Riding Hood?"

"To Grandmother's."

"What are you carrying under your apron?"

"Cake and medicine. My grandmother is sick and weak, and this will help her get well."

"Where does your grandmother live, Little Red Riding Hood?"

"Just outside the forest. Her house is under the three big oak trees. You can tell it by the hazel bushes," said Little Red Riding Hood.

The wolf thought to himself, "This soft young girl will be a juicy treat. She'll taste even better than the old woman. I'll have to be real clever if I want to catch them both." He kept walking next to Little Red Riding Hood, and after a while he said, "Little Red Riding Hood, just look at the beautiful flowers that are growing all around you! Wouldn't your grandmother love some lovely flowers?"

Little Red Riding Hood looked around and saw how the rays of the sun were dancing through the trees.

The woods were full of beautiful flowers.

So she thought to herself,

"If I take Grandmother a bunch of fresh flowers, she'd certainly like that. It's still early, if I quickly pick some flowers, I can still reach her in time." So she ran off the path and plunged into the woods to look for flowers.

Each time she plucked one, she thought another looked even prettier and ran after it.

This way she went deeper and deeper into the forest.

But the wolf went straight to Little Red Riding Hood's grandmother's house and knocked on the door. "Who's there?"

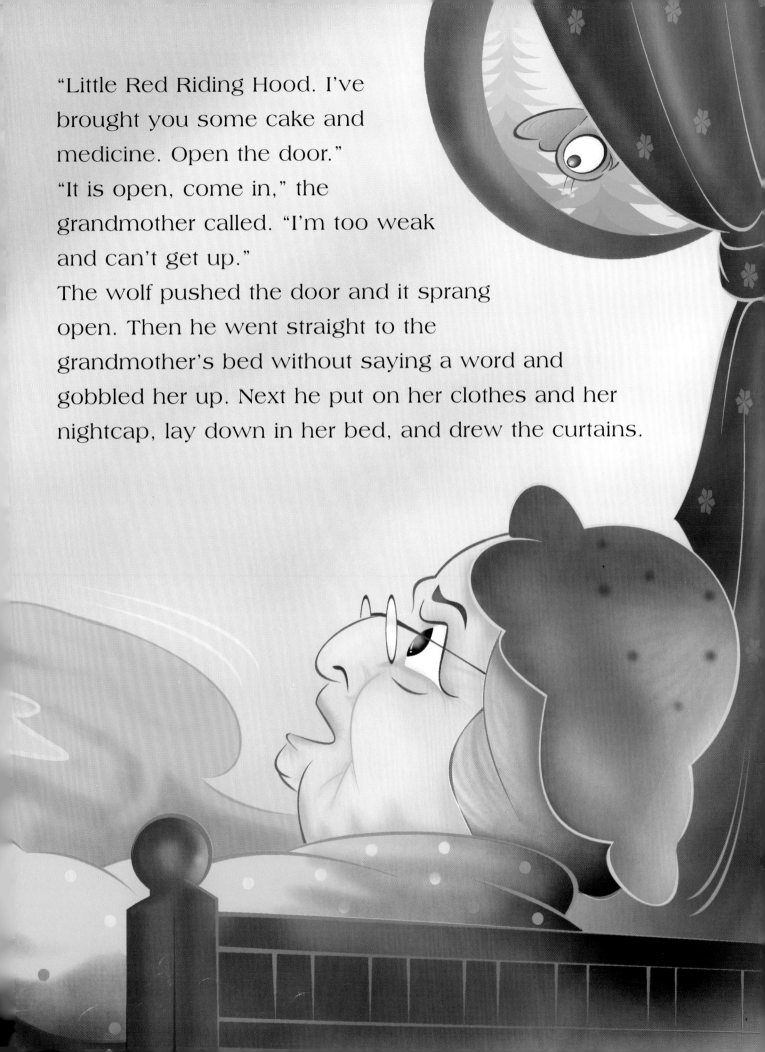

"Little Red Riding Hood. I've brought you some cake and medicine. Open the door."

"It is open, come in," the grandmother called. "I'm too weak and can't get up."

The wolf pushed the door and it sprang open. Then he went straight to the grandmother's bed without saying a word and gobbled her up. Next he put on her clothes and her nightcap, lay down in her bed, and drew the curtains.

Meanwhile, Little Red Riding Hood gathered as many flowers as she could carry. She remembered she had to go to her grandmother's house and ran all the way there. She was puzzled when she found the door open, and as she entered the room, it seemed so strange inside that she thought, "Oh, my God, how frightened I feel today, and usually I like to be at Grandmother's." She called out, "Good morning!" But she received no answer. Next she went to the bed and drew back the curtains.

There, lay her grandmother with her cap pulled down over her face, looking very strange indeed.

"Oh, Grandmother, what big ears you have!"
she exclaimed.

"The better to hear you with."

"Oh, Grandmother, what big hands you have!"

"The better to grab you with."

"Grandmother, what a terribly big mouth you have!"

"The better to eat you with."

No sooner did the wolf say that than he jumped out
of bed and gobbled up poor Little Red Riding
Hood. The wolf was so full, he lay
down in bed again, fell asleep
and began to snore very loudly.

A huntsman happened to be passing by
the house and thought to himself: "Why is
the old woman snoring so loudly? I better go
and see if everything is all right." He went into
the room, and when he came to the bed, he
saw the wolf lying on it.

"So I've found you at last, you wicked
wolf," said the huntsman. "I've been looking for
you for a long time."

He took aim with his gun and was about to shoot.

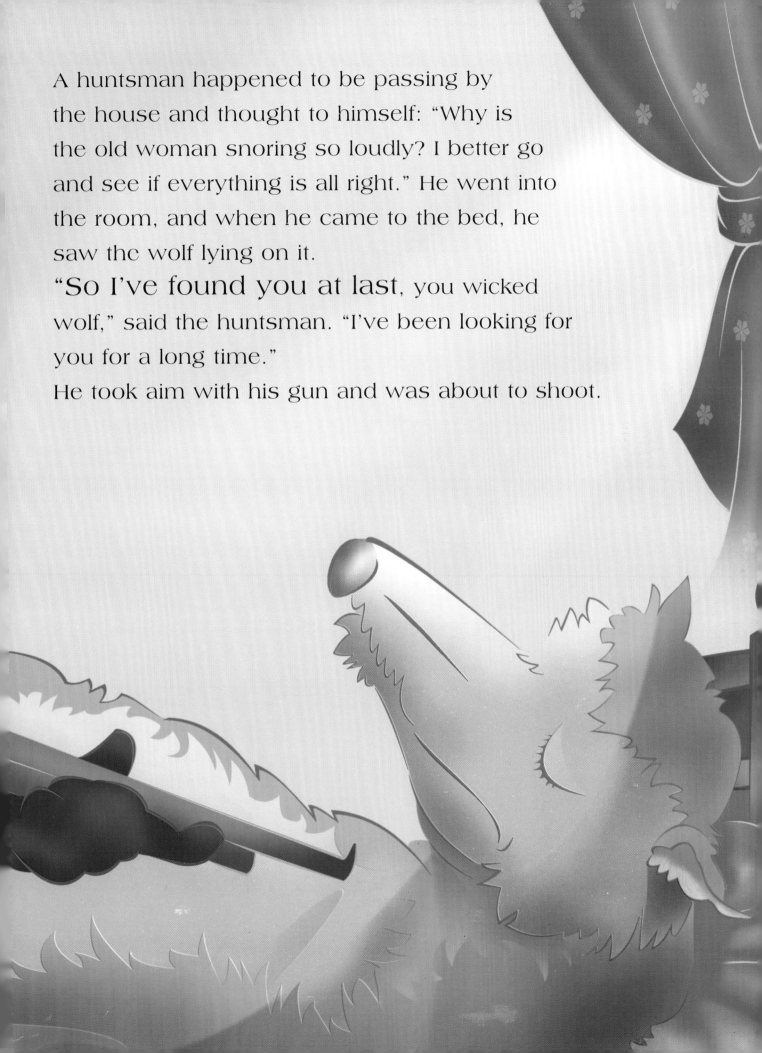

But then he thought that the wolf must
have eaten the grandmother and that
she could still be saved. So he did not
shoot but took some scissors and started
cutting open the sleeping wolf's belly.
After he made a couple of cuts, he saw little
Red Riding Hood's head and after he made a
few more cuts, the girl jumped out and exclaimed,
"Oh, how frightened I was! It was so dark in
the wolf's body."

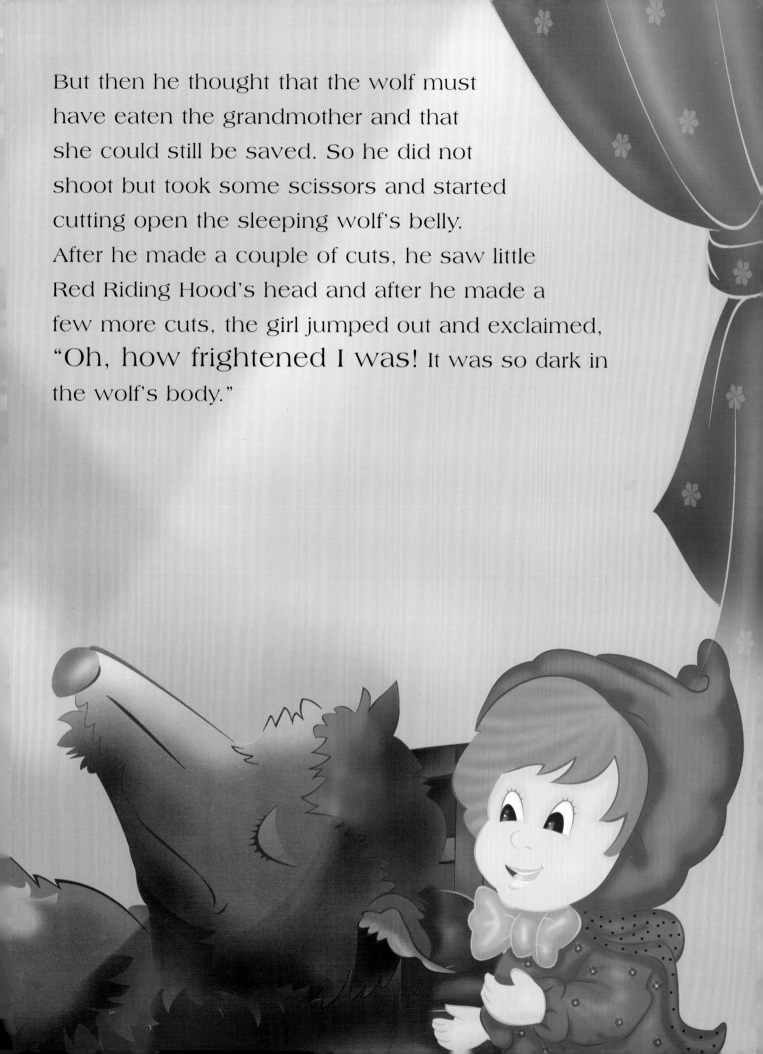

Soon the grandmother came out. She was alive but could hardly breathe. Little Red Riding Hood quickly brought some large stones, and they filled the wolf's belly with them. When he awoke and tried to run away, the stones were too heavy so he fell down.
"Now you wicked wolf, do you realize how bad you have been?" asked the huntsman.

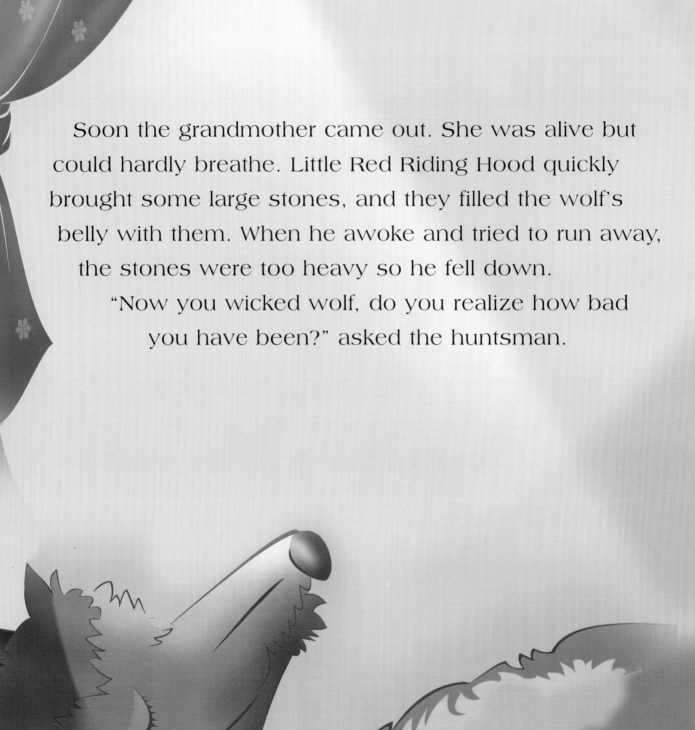

The wolf groaned.
"See, wolf, now you will
never be hungry so don't
eat anybody ever again. We will give
you food," said Little Red Riding Hood to him.
They all had a feast and soon Little Red Riding Hood was
on her way home again.